I0765546

SPECIAL THANKS TO:

Jason Zaiderman & family
for sponsoring this publication

Sarah Chyrek
for her beautiful illustrations

Lea Kron
for Graphic Design and Layout

CASTLE
Around My
Heart
Miriam Yerushalmi
Illustrated by Sarah Chyrek

721
719

"Come on, Devorah, can you walk a little faster? I don't want to be late just because you don't like school." Rochel sounded annoyed with her younger sister. Rochel frequently sounded annoyed with Devorah. "Every day you get slower and slower!"

"You can go on ahead of me," Devorah answered. "I don't mind. I'm not in a hurry."

"I wish I could go on without you, but Mommy said I have to make sure you get to class on time. Mrs. Hammer herself — you know, the principal," Rochel stressed the word, "the lady whose office you are always being sent to — called to say that your teacher won't let you in if you are late again. Nobody can take off to stay home with you, so please don't make any more problems for the rest of us!"

Devorah sighed quietly and began to walk more quickly to catch up. Rochel glanced back at her. "Why do you hate school so much, anyway?"

"Because school hates me!" Devorah burst out. "Every day I get picked on. On a good day, I'm only ignored. And that's just from my teacher! The other girls are even meaner. Some of them are really bullies!"

"Oh, Devorah, stop being so dramatic. It can't be that bad." Rochel looked at her sister sternly. "And if it is so terrible, maybe you are doing something wrong."

Devorah felt like crying, but she kept the tears in. The girls crossed the street and entered the school. Rochel walked with Devorah to her classroom. "I want to see you go inside," Rochel said. She put her hand on her sister's shoulder. "Try to have a good day, Devorah, ok?"

Devorah looked at Rochel without saying anything. Then she took a deep breath and opened the door.

Standing by the teacher's desk was a pleasant-looking woman Devorah had never seen before. "Good morning," the woman said. "Please take your seat and we will begin." Devorah hurried to her desk. Fortunately, she didn't trip over Ayala's foot that had somehow appeared in the aisle.

"Welcome, everyone. I am your new teacher, Morah Ehrlich."

Devorah and her classmates answered, "Good morning, Morah Ehrlich." The other girls began to whisper excitedly to each other. Morah Ehrlich waited calmly until they quieted down.

"Is everyone here now?" Morah Ehrlich noted that all the seats were filled. She opened her roll book. "When I call your name, please stand up and repeat your name,

as you wish to be called. For example, if I call Fraidy and you prefer Fraida, or if I call Miriam and you prefer Miri, now is the time to tell me."

Devorah felt a kick at the back of her chair. "Should we tell her what we prefer to call you?" Sarah whispered nastily. Vivi and Leah, who sat on either side of Sarah, snickered. Devorah sighed. Business as usual.

"I look forward to getting to know you all," Morah Ehrlich smiled at the class when roll call was finished. "Please take out your siddurim, and let's start davening."

She has a nice smile and a nice voice, Devorah thought. Maybe she'll really be nice. Devorah opened her siddur and began to daven from the depths of her heart. Please, Hashem, let this year turn out good, after all. Devorah was comforted by the opportunity to share

her troubles with Hashem. When she finished davening, Devorah kissed her siddur and closed it, feeling more hopeful than she had in a long time. Just then Morah Ehrlich said, "Please don't put your siddurim away yet, girls. I'd like you to open them up to page 12. Sarah, please read out loud what it says just before 'Mah Tovu'."

Sarah asked, "In Hebrew and English?"

"Yes, both."

Sarah read clearly, "Haraynee mekabel alai mitzvat asai shel ve'ahavta lerayacha kamocha. I hereby take upon myself the mitzvah of loving my fellow Jew as myself."

"Thank you, Sarah. Now, Vivi, please read the next pasuk (verse)."

Vivi hesitated, then read slowly, "Mah tovu oholecha Yaakov. How goodly are your tents, O Jacob."

"Thank you, Vivi," Morah Ehrlich said. "Girls, in the Nusach Ari siddurim, we read these two verses every morning. Why these particular statements, in this particular order?" She paused, looking around the classroom at the girls. "Leah, do you know who first uttered the verse 'How goodly are your tents'?"

Leah smiled a bit smugly before answering. "Of course, Morah. The evil prophet Bilaam had been hired by Balak, the Moabite king, to curse the Jewish people, but he was commanded by G-d to bless them instead."

"Very good, Leah. Can anyone tell us why this statement would be a blessing? Devorah?" Muffled laughter broke out from a few of the students. Devorah heard someone whisper —loudly enough for Morah Ehrlich to hear also — "She won't know!"

Trying not to sound nervous, Devorah said, "Well, we learned that 'How goodly are your tents' refers to the fact that in the wilderness, the Bnei Yisrael arranged their tents so that none of the entrances would face each other; this way no one would be able to see into his neighbor's home."

Morah Ehrlich smiled. "Exactly right, Devorah. According to the Baal Shem Tov, 'not looking into one's neighbor's tent,' into their home, means that the Jews did not scrutinize their neighbors' faults. Why is the mitzvah

of loving our fellow Jew stated before this prayer? Because the way you develop ahavas Yisrael, the way you come to love your friend as you love yourself, is by not looking at their faults. Instead, try to focus on their good points."

She paused. "You've heard of Rav Mendel Futerfas?" Some of the students nodded. "Rav Futerfas, zt"l, taught Torah in Russia, in secret schools, which was a crime there. He was caught and sent to prison. While he was in jail, he noticed that the inmates in the cell across from him passed the time playing cards. Rav Futerfas knew that prisoners weren't allowed to have cards or any other entertainment. The guards also noticed, and kept trying to confiscate the cards. Strangely, though, whenever they entered that cell, the cards were nowhere to be found. The guards eventually gave up and left those prisoners alone.

"Rav Futerfas couldn't contain his curiosity. 'How do you always manage to hide the cards?' he asked them. The men laughed. 'We're thieves,' one of them explained, 'and quick with our hands. Whenever the guard comes in, we hide the cards in his own pocket. Before he goes out again, we take them back.' Rav Futerfas was astonished at their audacity, but even more surprised that the guards never thought to look in their own pockets."

The teacher looked around at each girl.

"So often, we don't look in our own pockets, either. We tend to look at everyone else's faults and get annoyed with them. But, we only need to focus on looking in our own tents, and work on ourselves. Realize that no one is perfect — not me, not you. Only Hashem is perfect."

"Oh, Hashem, please," Devorah thought, "let my classmates remember this lesson and take it to heart!"

"With that in mind, girls," Morah Ehrlich said, "let's put away our siddurim and take out our Chumashim, please."

Devorah noticed that throughout the rest of the morning's lessons, her classmates were uncharacteristically well-behaved. They hardly bothered her at all — when the teacher was looking. Devorah was almost sorry when the lunch bell rang.

"Please line up at the door," Morah Ehrlich announced.

While the other girls moved quickly to stand near their friends, Devorah walked slowly to the end of the line. As she drew near, some of the other girls moved away.

"Don't stand so close to me," Leah muttered. "Haven't you heard about 'personal space'?"

The daily routine had not changed. In the lunchroom, as usual, Devorah sat at the far end of the table. As usual, no one passed her the serving plates. Devorah didn't even ask for anything anymore. As the other girls were about to take second helpings, though, Morah Ehrlich quietly asked Vivi to pass the food to Devorah.

"Of course, Morah, I was just about to do that," she responded, but behind the teacher's back, Vivi made a face. She picked up the bowl and plopped it down nearer Devorah but just out of her reach.

The students ate and cleared away their plates

quickly, eager to start recess. Devorah ate slowly, intending to stay at the table as long as possible. She took a book out of her pocket and began to read.

"It's a beautiful day outside, girls, let's all go enjoy it," Morah Ehrlich said.

"Oh, Morah Ehrlich, Devorah always stays inside," Sarah said, sweetly. "We used to ask her to join us but she never wanted to."

"If the class is going somewhere, the whole class is going," Morah Ehrlich said firmly. "Please finish up and join us on line, Devorah."

"Don't try to play with us outside, either," Leah sneered in a harsh whisper.

"I wouldn't think of it," Devorah responded quietly.

"Well, of course you wouldn't think…" Leah and Vivi laughed. Devorah turned red. She held her book tightly and reluctantly followed her classmates into the yard.

Morah Ehrlich was standing by the door, watching the girls play.

"What are you reading, Devorah?" she asked, as Devorah came down the steps. "Oh, that was one of my favorites!" the teacher exclaimed when she saw the title. "I'd love to talk about it with you sometime."

Devorah looked around the schoolyard. Sarah, Leah, and Vivi had stopped playing ball. They were watching her. They didn't look happy. Devorah opened her book, but she didn't start reading. Maybe she should ask Morah Ehrlich to just leave her alone? Didn't she realize that the nicer she was to Devorah, the meaner her classmates would be?

Morah Ehrlich noticed the olive tree growing in the corner of the schoolyard. "How nice to have such a tree right here!" she said to the girls playing near her. "Have you ever seen how olive oil is made, girls? The olives are crushed under tremendous pressure—and that precious oil is the result. It's amazing what good can come out of seemingly painful experiences."

At the end of the day, Devorah waited outside for Rochel. Sarah, Leah, and Vivi passed her on their way home. "Well, look who's still here. Are you hoping to walk home with Morah Ehrlich or something?" Sarah asked mockingly. "Just because we have one new teacher, don't think anything has changed. She'll be on our side pretty soon, you'll see. Bye, bye!"

Rochel came out in time to see the three girls walk away laughing. "So, how was your day? Not bad, right? Your friends seem happy."

"I wouldn't exactly call those girls my friends," Devorah said, "but it actually was a pretty good day, baruch Hashem. We—"

Rochel cut her off. "See, I knew you were exaggerating. Maybe you're picking up some social skills after all. Listen, I have a big test tomorrow, so I'm going to Binah's house to study with her. I'll call Mommy from there. Be careful on the way home, ok?" Rochel waved goodbye and left with her friend.

Devorah walked home by herself, thinking over the day's events.

"Devorah, I'm happy to hear you were on time for school this morning. Please, let's keep it up," her mother greeted her when she got home.

"We have a new teacher in the morning," Devorah told her mother.

"That's nice. You can tell us about it at dinner, ok? Please set the table while I get the little ones washed up and changed. Thank you, Devorah." Her mother hurried out of the room. But at dinner, Devorah didn't talk about her day. She was sure that telling her family how difficult school had become for her, with all the bullying that went on, would just be too stressful for them. So, Devorah had decided to keep it to herself.

But she was beginning to think she wasn't handling it very well.

Devorah got ready for school quickly the next morning. Rochel was surprised that Devorah was keeping up with her as they walked together. "What happened?" she asked. "Do you have a class trip today?"

"No," Devorah replied, "I just don't want us to be late. Don't you have a big test this morning?"

"Yes," Rochel said, "and I still need to review one question with my friends before class starts. I don't really have time to walk you to your classroom. You'll go straight there, won't you?"

"Yes, I will," Devorah said. She hoped Rochel wouldn't notice how was anxious she was to see if Morah Ehrlich would be there again.

Devorah was relieved to find the new teacher at her desk. During davening, Devorah again opened her heart to Hashem. Please, please, Hashem, let this year be better; let this teacher be really nice; let the other girls stop being mean.

"Let's review Navi now," Morah Ehrlich said after davening. "There are so many messages we can learn from Dovid HaMelech. Many situations in Dovid's life seemed 'bad' or like mistakes, yet good came from all of them. For example, Dovid was an outcast to his family throughout his childhood and youth; they did not accept him until he was 28 years old. What good do you think

came from that?"

Morah Ehrlich listened to the girls' suggested answers.

"Those are all very thoughtful responses," she commented sincerely. "Another possible answer is that Hashem wanted Dovid to be a good king, and a good king needs to have the middah, the character trait, of anavah, humility. Many people in Dovid's situation would grow bitter and try to build themselves up by putting others down. Dovid HaMelech never did that. He didn't get angry at others or upset at his circumstances. He worked on his middos. Dovid, like Yaakov Avinu and Moshe Rabbeinu, was a shepherd for many years. They spent so much of their time alone outside, and while caring for

the flocks, they worked on elevating themselves."

The teacher wondered if her students really understood the point she was trying to make.

"Girls," she continued, "who do we spend most of our time with?"

Esther raised her hand. "With our friends?"

Nechamah Dinah asked, "With our family?"

"With our teachers!" Fraida piped up.

Everyone laughed, even Devorah.

"I don't spend time with friends or family. I spend most of my time by myself," Devorah thought to herself, as she picked up her pencil and started doodling mindlessly on the notebook page in front of her. "Actually, class, we spend most of our time with… ourselves."

Devorah dropped her pencil. As she leaned over to pick it up, Leah whispered, "Who else would want to spend time with you?"

Devorah felt the anger and sadness growing inside her, until she thought she would explode at Leah, and Vivi, and Sarah, and all the other girls who tormented

RULES
About Me:

her. Fortunately, Morah Ehrlich's calm voice cut through her pain.

"When Dovid HaMelech danced with joy in front of the Aron HaKodesh, the Holy Ark, his wife Michal criticized him for behaving without the proper honor befitting a king. Did Dovid allow her words to change him? Did he change his behavior, his thinking, his mood, because of her displeasure? No. He continued to express his happiness in the way he felt was right. Dovid HaMelech always had the ability to find the positive in a difficult situation."

Morah Ehrlich sat down. "Let's look inside the Navi and see if that ability is applied in this perek."

Devorah thought about this lesson often over the next few days. Was her life more difficult than Dovid HaMelech's life had been? Would she be able to find the positive in her circumstances, if she tried? Maybe only someone as great as Dovid HaMelech could do that. But could pushing herself to find the positive be the very thing that would make her great?

She wondered about this during lunch, when Morah Ehrlich again had to instruct someone to pass the food to her; during recess, when too many balls were "accidentally" kicked into her book; during afternoon class, when she faced the usual nasty comments and looks. She thought about it on her walk home with Rochel, through dinner, and when she went to bed at night.

That Shabbos, Devorah was still thinking about it. In the afternoon, when her parents were resting, Devorah

took her younger siblings to the park. She sat down on a bench that gave her a good view of the play area. She became so involved in her thoughts that she was startled to hear someone calling her name.

"Good Shabbos, Devorah! It's so nice to see you!" Morah Ehrlich was saying.

"Oh — good Shabbos," Devorah stammered out. "I'm here with my little sisters and brothers."

"Yes, it's such good weather, we had to come out. There are my boys climbing the slide," Morah Ehrlich said. She gestured at the bench on which Devorah was sitting. "Would you mind if I joined you?"

"Of course not!" Devorah sat up a bit straighter.

They watched the little children play for a few minutes. Devorah sat quietly, feeling very shy, while Morah Ehrlich commented on the children's antics. Suddenly Devorah decided to take a chance. "Morah, may I ask you something?"

"Certainly, Devorah, I'd be happy to answer if I can."

"When you were talking about being positive when things seem bad — can everyone do that? Maybe Dovid HaMelech didn't feel bad about the way people treated him, but I do."

"That's a good question," the teacher answered. "Yes, people can develop a more positive attitude about their circumstances. Dovid HaMelech understood that everything is from Hashem, and that Hashem has a reason for everything He does. When you understand this, it will help you feel more positive, too. There are so many possible reasons why someone might treat another person badly. One might be that they are struggling with some challenge in their life, and they may be lashing out

at others from their pain."

Devorah said slowly, "So you're saying that the girls who are so mean to me might be the ones who have a problem? The nasty things they say or do to me, really have nothing to do with me?"

"Exactly. You are not the cause of their pain, you're just a convenient target. The more we understand that it's about them and not about us, the more we're free not to be hurt by them. You'll see how this protects us."

Just then one of Morah Ehrlich's sons tumbled off the slide. She went over to help him up and give him a hug. When she returned to their bench, Devorah asked, "What do you mean, 'protects us'? Should I come to school with a bodyguard?"

"Actually," the teacher said, "in a way, you should. Just like a king puts guards around his castle, to protect his family, you can learn how to put up guards around your 'castle'— your heart. The Torah tells us (Deut. 16:18), 'Shoftim veshotrim titein lecha bechol she'orecha, Judges and guards you shall appoint in all your gates.' This teaches us many lessons. Literally, it means you have to protect yourself and your property, physically, with strong walls and watchmen. It also can mean to protect yourself spiritually and emotionally. 'Mikol mishmor netzor libecha ki mimenu totzos chaim, Above all else, guard your heart, for all life flows from it' (Proverbs 4:23)."

"How can I do that? What kinds of guards can I put around my heart?" Devorah wondered.

"Our eyes, our ears, our mouth — these are all gates that protect our heart and soul. Torah wisdom is like guards posted at the gates, protecting us from being

harmed by others. With Torah wisdom we can guard what we see, hear, and say. But Torah guards work both ways: they also help us judge more favorably — to see the good in others, hear what people are really trying to say, and speak with kindness."

"I like that idea," Devorah responded. "But I think it will still hurt when people are mean to me."

"Well, it takes time to build this castle around your heart. When you learn to trust the guards, though, it will be easier to look past the nasty words and even to have compassion on those who just don't know yet how to overcome their yetzer hara."

Devorah began to feel hopeful.

Morah Ehrlich continued, "We all want to be liked, we all want people to appreciate our good qualities. Your job is to be aware of your own beautiful qualities and love yourself, and that way you will be able to love others." Morah Ehrlich smiled at her student. "Always remember that you are a very precious princess — you are a daughter of the King of Kings, who loves you very much! That is a guard in itself."

"I'll think about that," Devorah said. "I'll try not to take what they say so much to heart— or," she gave a little smile, "into my castle."

"Just remember, Torah wisdom is boundless and provides all kinds of guards.

Knowing that those girls are letting their yetzer hara control them is one guard, knowing that Hashem loves you is another, and knowing that you love yourself is a third," Mrs. Ehrlich repeated. "Your family who loves you is another guard, too, even if you don't always see it."

Devorah nodded. "I almost feel bad for those girls now. Morah, how do you know so much about this?"

"These are some of the things that helped me when I was being bullied."

Devorah stared at her teacher.

"Yes, Devorah, I also had a tough time when I was younger. But I had some wonderful teachers who helped me. That's what made me want to become a teacher myself."

Devorah smiled. "Maybe after I finish building my castle, I'll become a teacher too, some day."

Morah Ehrlich smiled too. "Just don't forget that you are, and will always be, a princess. If you need a reminder, just give me a call."

At recess she sat under the tree with her book and began to read. Her concentration was interrupted by some loud whispering nearby.

"She forgot. Can you believe that? My own mother forgot my birthday? I'm so upset!"

"Well, maybe she'll surprise you with a cake or a present tonight."

"Not likely. There's so much going on right now at home. I understand she's really swamped, and I don't feel right mentioning it to her. But it still hurts."

Devorah kept her eyes down, but she noticed Fraida walking by with Miriam, who looked on the edge of tears. Neither Miriam nor Fraida had ever actually been nasty to her, but they had never been very friendly, either. They just sort of ignored her. Nonetheless, Devorah felt very

bad for Miriam.

Devorah was thoughtful when she left school that day. She saw Miriam and Fraida waving goodbye to each other before they started off in opposite directions. Impulsively, Devorah ran up to Fraida.

"Wait, Fraida," Devorah said. "Can I talk to you for a minute?"

"Me? What do you want to talk to me about? And we'll have to talk as we walk, I need to go straight home."

"I didn't mean to, but I overheard part of your conversation with Miriam during recess. Is she still upset?"

"Well, it's not really your business," Fraida answered. "Why do you want to know?"

"I can understand how she feels," Devorah said, "and I wanted to do something to cheer her up. You're her best friend. I would need your help."

"That's nice of you," Fraida said slowly. "I'm surprised. I never would have thought of you taking the initiative like this."

"I'm a little surprised myself." Devorah began speaking as the two girls crossed the street. "I was thinking we could make Miriam a surprise party in school, or at your house? You'll have to tell her mother about it right away. Maybe call and ask if she minds if we do this — that way, she'll remember about Miriam's birthday, hopefully before Miriam says anything."

"That's a good idea!" Fraida said admiringly. "Baruch Hashem, I usually get home a little before Miriam does. I'll call right away." Then she surprised Devorah by asking, "Why don't you come home with me now, so we can work this out?"

BIRTHDAY

"So, do you think it would be ok to have the party at your house?" Devorah asked.

Fraida shook her head. "Not on such short notice. I think it would be best to have it in school, but we'd need permission."

"Maybe — maybe we could ask Morah Ehrlich?"

"Maybe you could ask Morah Ehrlich!" Fraida smiled at Devorah. "She seems to like you — and I'm beginning to understand why."

They reached Fraida's house. "I'll call Miriam's mother, then you can call home if you need to let anyone know where you are," Fraida stated. "Then, call Morah Ehrlich."

"Miriam's mother sounded really grateful," Fraida reported. "She remembered she has a cake in the freezer, she'll decorate it and serve it for dessert." She handed the phone to Devorah, who called home and left a short message, and then nervously dialed her teacher's number.

"Oh, hello, Devorah," the teacher answered. "Is

everything ok?"

"Yes, Morah Ehrlich, baruch Hashem, it's fine, that is, I'm fine, but we — Fraida and I — need to ask you something." She took a deep breath and explained the situation quickly.

"What a lovely idea! Of course, you have my permission to have the party during recess, and even a little longer! I'll send Miriam on an errand to give you a chance to set up." Devorah smiled delightedly with relief. Before she hung up, the teacher said, "Devorah, this is truly something a princess would think of."

Fraida brought some drinks and snacks to the table. "Let's start calling the other girls now."

"You'd better make those calls," Devorah sighed, "if anyone hears my voice, they'll probably hang up."

Fraida blushed and said, "Ok." She spoke to her classmates for what seemed like hours, while Devorah checked names off the class list and took notes on what each girl would contribute. Finally, Fraida put the phone down. "Well, everybody knows what to bring tomorrow and what the plan is. With Hashem's help, it could really be good!"

Devorah stood up. "I guess I'd better get home now. Thanks so much, Fraida."

"Thank you, Devorah. And Miriam thanks you too — even though she doesn't know it yet!" Grinning, Fraida walked Devorah to the door. "You know, I think things in our class are going to be a lot different for you, in a good way, after tomorrow."

And baruch Hashem, they were.

CHILDREN'S BOOKS BY MIRIAM YERUSHALMI

Available on Amazon.com

*Also available in
Hebrew & Yiddish*

*Also available in
Hebrew & Yiddish*

*Also available in
Hebrew & Yiddish*

*Also available
in Yiddish*

*Also available
in Yiddish*

*Also available
in Yiddish*

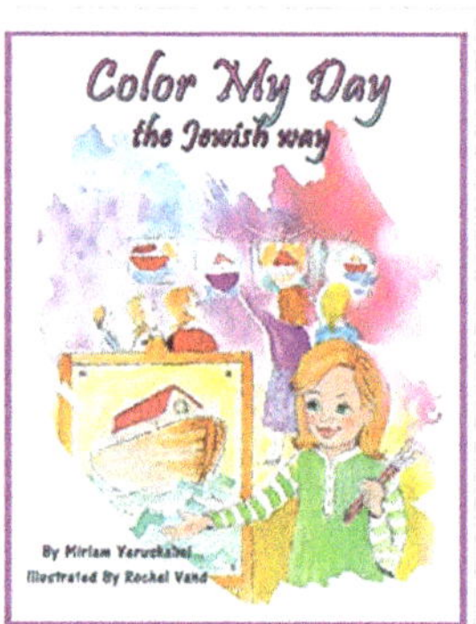

*Also available
in Yiddish*

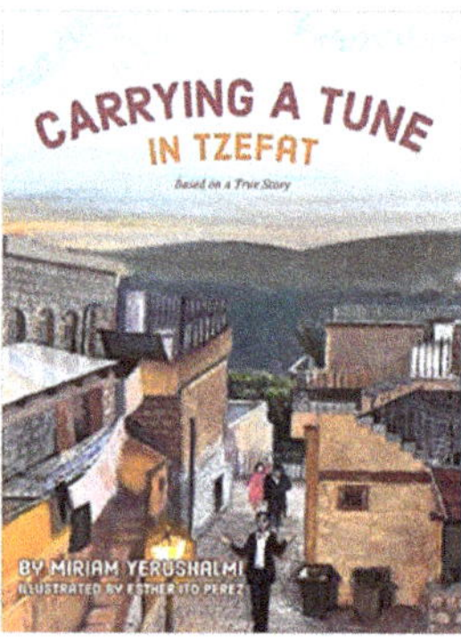

*Also available
in Yiddish*

*Also available
in Yiddish*

*Also available
in Yiddish*

*Also available
in Spanish*

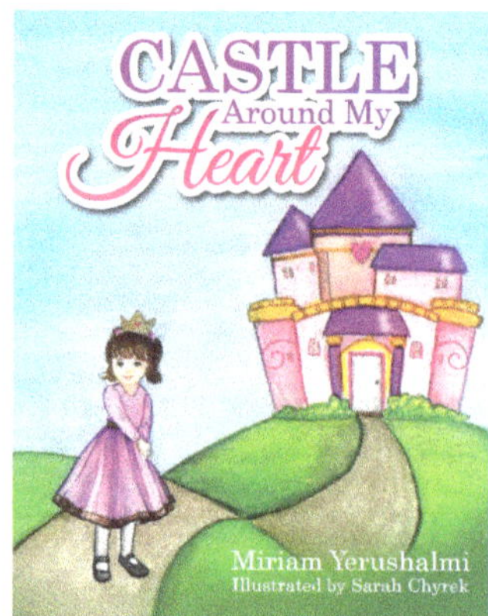

ADULT BOOKS BY MIRIAM YERUSHALMI

Available on Amazon.com

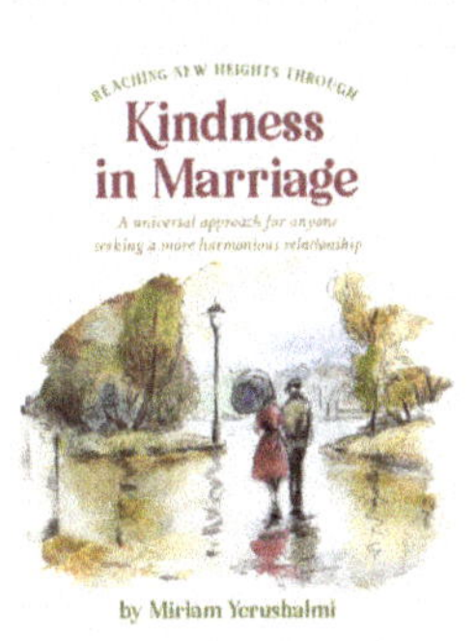  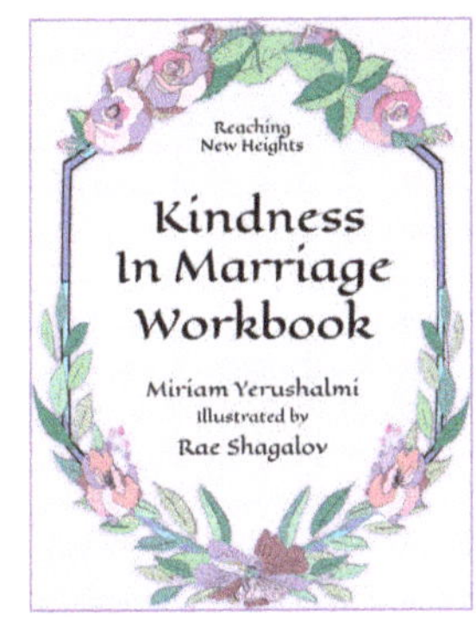

COMING SOON:

Chaim Becomes a True Prince

Yossi's New Normal

Brain Train

Bais Hamikdash Within

Reaching New Heights Through Healthier Cooking

Reaching New Heights Through Living Tanya

ABOUT THE AUTHOR

Miriam Yerushalmi has a MA degree in Psychology and Marriage and Family Counseling. She has worked extensively with children for over 40 years, creating brain training programs to teach self-regulation through drama, dance and the arts.